I0621307

OVER A BARREL:

The Phalanx Blood Series Part II

BRUCE E. ARRINGTON

Paisley, Oregon

My blood kills cancer.

Yep, you read that right. The big bad *C* word that scares just about everyone these days. My blood kills it. *Dead. Dead Kennedys'* invitation to the White House dead. Disappointed George Romero dead. Doesn't matter what type of cancer. It quickly finds itself outmaneuvered, surrounded, and mercilessly crushed by an iron-red phalanx. Just a few drops of my blood—*drops* mind you, and miracles start happening.

It's been what—nine or ten weeks now since this all began? After I turned 16, I agreed to my parents' wishes and donated blood to the Red Cross. They of course rewarded me with some virtual reality awesomeness, so I was happy to help. Charity is its own reward, you know?

Some folks at the Red Cross lab found out that the titer levels were somewhere between Neptune and Pluto, and they couldn't keep quiet about it. (Yes, I know you astronomers out there will tell me Pluto isn't a "planet" anymore, but a man has to take a stand when his childhood is at stake. Pluto will always be a planet in my heart, dagnabbit; I *believe* in it, same as the brontosaurus. And paleontologists ate a pterodactyl's worth of crow finally acknowledging that one!) One person told another and they told twenty more and soon, well, I don't know how many were involved, but probably a lot. Too many. Someone had the bright idea to test it on *cancer* cells.

And...***bingo***. My life changes overnight; for the good, or so I thought. It looked like I was gonna ride a rocket to the big time. Like I'd get real rich, be a big super hero and save lots of people from miserable pain and suffering.

You've heard the old saying "The best laid plans of mice and men…" right? Well, don't forget the rest of it—the part that certainly came true for me: "…often go awry."

Thanks, Robert Burns. I don't know if you jinxed me or what. For the non-literary, when one rides a rocket be cautious where the point sticks.

Soon after, my mom was beat up at work (the same day she was *fired*—oh yeah, great day that was). I was kidnapped by one of the pharm companies, and my personal world view changed. Dramatically.

I don't hate everyone on planet Earth. Please don't misunderstand. I've had a pretty good life so far. There are some good people who have contributed to my welfare these 16 years. My mom and dad, grandmas and grandpas and cousins and other family members, and friends I've grown up with. But there *are* bad people who want what I have, like jealous researchers whose life ambition is to be the top dog in their field, and they don't care who they have to hurt to get there. Ironic, isn't it? Aren't they supposed to be helping people instead of hurting them?

But when they come after me and people I love, I won't stand for it.

For now Mom and Dad are off on a well-deserved vacation (for their protection), far away from here. I haven't talked with them yet, though I really miss them. The time isn't right, and it definitely isn't safe.

My friends—who in this document I call Michael, Charlie and Courtney in lieu of their real names to shield them from any backlash it may create—rescued me by starting a fire where I was being held prisoner and drained of my cancer-killing blood. (Later I learn that blaze took out most of the building. No regrets there.) They even helped set up my new living space.

I've had some time to think, plan, and put a good part of my *Phalanx blood* money to good use. Time will tell if my suspicions play out.

But time isn't exactly on my side. The pharm companies that took my blood will be needing more. Soon. Apparently my blood can't be duplicated. Yet. That's what Charlie told me.

Oh yeah, so get this: these real smart CEOs stand in front of the world, claiming *they* discovered a cancer cure. Yay them. And of course their stock goes way up. But just watch what happens when all the lies bite 'em back. The entire world's eyes are on them and their promise to rid it of the plague scourging millions. They won't have long to make good; people can't afford to be patient. The pressure is going to skyrocket, and it won't bleed off unless they can find me, which isn't happening. I am their cure. There is nothing else. See why they want me so badly? It ain't for my pleasant personality.

So, to recap, the pharm companies learned my blood cells kill cancer. One won a contract to buy regular blood samples, and their competitors kidnapped me. I was rescued by friends and escaped. Me, their only source for the cure, and they can't touch me. For now.

*

I wake in a cold sweat as snatches of a savage dream fade from my mind. And I do mean savage—it isn't pretty. I'm strapped down; lights blind me, and I can only see the vague spiderlike silhouette of machine arms. Before ice-cold fear can churn through my gut at the thought of what wicked instruments tip those arms a huge syringe dips from on high. It's so long I can't see the plunger at the rear. It is shoved into my comparatively small arm. Suddenly, not just blood but everything gets sucked (slurped?) into the syringe. My whole arm shrivels, leaving only bone.

That's all that's left of the current nightmare. You think that's gross? You should have seen my dreams while I was kept prisoner for almost five weeks. Those make even *Deadpool* look tame.

I haven't slept restfully since coming to my new meager apartment. Not to sound ungrateful but my old bedroom is bigger than this entire place. But when I first got here I was beyond exhaustion and did not care where I lay my head. Michael swore I crashed for 18 hours straight. My friends watched over me and went shopping for essentials. I owe them big time.

It took a while for the drugs to wear off and build enough energy to sit up for an hour before falling over and going back to sleep. It wouldn't matter what position you put me in, either. I'd follow gravity where it took me and the lights went out. Whenever I woke up it was hard to think of anything but my next nap, where more nightmares awaited. Blood, muscles, and sometimes guts. Running from someone, some…thing. And it wasn't always human.

And now here I sit, dressed and ready, in the apartment on my school campus. It's Monday morning and my study time will soon begin. Only a few people know I'm here since I can't roam freely anymore. My tutor is one of them. Up 'til now he's been okay, but he acts sort of weasely. No, not a ginger in hand-me-downs with parents who don't know the meaning of the words "birth control." *That* Weasely I actually like and would probably be a better teacher. But no, this guy is oily, shifty, sneaky, *and* not straight with me. So I call him Wease, just not to his face; weasels can be nasty if you tick them off. He was hired by Charlie's dad, who knows about my predicament. He supposedly funded my escape from the prison of blood suckers, and arranged for my stay here. But he used to be on the board of the company that got me into all this trouble. See how that can be a conflict of interest? I don't have any proof he's up to no good. Yet.

So, do I feel safe in this place? Kind of, but only because the school bodyguard knows I'm here. You know, the built Irish WWE pinup I told you about last time. She stopped the three suits who chased me.

She's. So. Hot.

It's not that I'm into her looks, either. Okay, she's nice to look at. But there's more. It's her style, the attitude she holds when something big comes at her. It's like: *Okay, bring it on. Let's see what you can do.* Sheer awesomeness when she twists her foes like a pretzel. Like the older sister I always wanted.

Scratch that. It would be really creepy if I had those feelings about my older sister.

*

I hear this rapid *tap-tap-tap* on my door, as if it's a secret code or something. Then it repeats. Is this his idea of a joke? I look through the window. Looks like Wease, and not many can duplicate his facial features, so I let him in.

My tutor is tall and lanky, in his early twenties, wears oversized glasses, and a sports jacket a couple of years (or maybe a decade) beyond its lifetime. A perpetual smug grin dominates his lower face, while beady eyes rule the rest. The only positive here is he knows his stuff: math, science, history, English. You name it, he knows it. And he knows he knows it, though I've been able to stump him a time or two during Greek history lessons. And ethics. Turns out I know a few things he doesn't. Go figure.

Wease saunters in, drops his heavy backpack on the small table coffee, and stretches with a yawn. Yeah, real professional. As usual he wanders around the small apartment, peering mostly at the wall outlets and smoke detectors, and nothing else in particular. I wonder if he's looking for the latest layer of dust to inspect, or a new spider web to probe. Is he grading me on my inability to keep the apartment clean? He strikes me as a man who subjects all the world to intense scrutiny but has a blind spot when it comes to mirrors, else he'd be more aware of his own weaknesses where it comes to his lack of chin and inability to stand up straight.

But I just open my textbook and wait for him, sighing and wishing he'd hurry his inspection up. Algebra II is first since it tends to rob me of my brain energy. So I get it out of the way early.

Finally Wease comes back and sits.

"Have you calculated the square footage of your apartment yet?" he asks, out of the blue. *Yet?* I've just finished sleeping, sweating, and shivering out whatever my captors were shooting me up with, let alone thought about decorating the place. The walls, the carpet, the furniture, the kitchenette and coffin-sized bathroom, it's all the same beige blah that's reached by committee you get in expensive gated housing associations and state-run asylums. I think it would be easy to answer if I possessed the right measuring tools, or the asinine impulse.

"No reason to depress myself unnecessarily," I reply, keeping my tone in check. Don't want to tick off the tutor yet. It's only the second week.

"Hmmm..." he continues, pausing, as if he has all the time in the world. He disappears for a quick minute into my small bedroom and bathroom, and reappears with a calculating look on his face. "I'd say between 450 and 475 square feet." He looks at me as if waiting for my nodding approval. But I don't give it. I'm tired of this game. It's so obvious he is scoping out my place.

But *why*?

I play dumb so I just shrug and look back at today's assigned lesson.

"It was really kind of Charlie's dad to set you up here," Wease goes on. This is like a repeat of our first day. Like, you have great friends, Bernard (not my real name), like I should be ever so grateful. Isn't everyone so kind to you?

Is this supposed to endear me to Charlie's dad? What am I, five years old?

"I'm trying to factor these polynomials of degree 4," I respond, trying to get him to focus. "I need you to check this one."

Typically Wease has a one track mind, such that until I address whatever he is focused on, he doesn't switch topics. At least not unless forced to. Suddenly I see that his one-track mind is actually trying to jump into an adjacent lane, with the result of his mind-car (if he had one) swerving all over his mind-map head, attempting to refocus. It isn't pretty but he finally manages to sit down and nod. And finally we do math.

Fast forward to our "break." He likes to take 15 minutes between subjects, when he walks outside, makes phone calls, smokes a pipe, whatever. I'm not able to monitor his calls, as he's too far away, hidden behind a tree somewhere. Not that I really care, but this time his voice sounds loud and urgent. Either like arguing-with-girlfriend urgent, or not-wanting-to-do-something urgent. Admittedly, I have more experience with the latter than the former. But, again, I don't care. I have my own problems and I've got my Greek history text open. Time is burning. Tick-tock. The quicker we get the lessons done the sooner he leaves.

I overhear his nasally tone just before he opens the door. It sounds resigned to something inevitable.

"Fine, see you in a few." He comes in and I play ignorant with my nose in my book. If I ask any questions about what his phone conversation was about, it'll likely take an hour for him to make up another good lie, and afterward we'll still have to get back on the school track.

Great. We have company today. I think I have an idea who he talked to so I stealthily send out a couple of texts while he re-inspects the apartment. Again?

What is he doing? Could there be hidden cameras or mics in here? Is that what the phone call was all about? Was he arguing with someone because he wasn't doing his job properly, whatever his real job is supposed to be? My imagination goes into overdrive thinking of the negative possibilities. Sometimes I do that when I'm stressed, and all sorts of conspiracy theories flood my brain cells.

And 99.9 percent of the time I'm dead wrong. Just ask my old girlfriend, my parents, and my friends. I usually end up eating so much crow that I can imitate all their grating coos, caws, rattles, and clicks.

But I can't shake my suspicions this time, with Wease acting this way. It takes me a while to focus after he finally sits down and we are into the lesson about Danaus and the Danaids, who murdered their new husbands. Yay, go girls.

About twenty minutes later there's a light rap on the door. This time it's Charlie's dad, coming for a nice friendly visit, or so I hope. The man is short, bulging, with a light complexion and balding reddish hair. He apologizes for interrupting the lessons, but his tone suggests it's a minor issue since he's clearly present on more important business. He sets a brown tattered briefcase on the floor by the table and takes a quick look around the place, and glances at the *same* wall outlets and *same* smoke detectors that Wease always inspects. And that's when my suspicions are confirmed.

My heart sinks to the floor.

They're spying on me.

Hidden cameras can look like just about anything these days, and now I'm cursing my stupidity for not considering this possibility. But at the time, I was dog-tired and thought of little else but hiding and sleep. Eating came later once my appetite returned.

A disturbing awareness settles on me.

Wease. Walked. Into. My. Bedroom. And. My. Bathroom.

Realizing that my privacy has been fully exploited, I find it hard to focus on Greek mythology, or anything other than offering both of them coffee and making sure they get artificial sweetener so tumors pop up in twenty years, provided they move to California.

I don't care to know what they saw or heard. I just want them out of here.

Like, an hour ago.

But somehow I manage to provide something other than a death face. And since Charlie's dad isn't even looking directly at me, it's not likely he suspects I know anything.

He smiles; it's better than a used salesman. With the money he earns in a year, it better be. "So, you're feeling better?" he says hurriedly. "Nice place, right?"

I barely nod. *Think about Greek history*, I tell myself. *The men all murdered on their wedding nights. Focus on anything instead of the fact that these two lowlifes invaded your personal space.*

Charlie's dad sits on the edge of the couch. He faces the table and stares holes into me. I look back at him and try to smile, but I can't.

"Is there something you needed?" I ask in my most frosty tone.

"Hmmm…me?" he says. "No, not really. Just glad you're safe and sound." He laughs. It's forced. No mirth reaches his face. "That fire set 'em back a few million dollars. Guess they got what they deserved."

Not quite, I think.

He snaps his fingers. "Hey, have you watched the news about…all this cancer stuff?"

I don't have a TV and the laptop the school loaned me can't get the internet since I'm too far from a wireless source.

Snark is reserved for friends, family, and the trustworthy. He therefore gets a polite no.

He continues without a beat. Yep, this is all rehearsed. "There's been all this uproar about the pharm companies taking too long to roll out their newly found cure." His eyebrows raise as he looks at me. "Now they've got demonstrators marching on their doorstep." He laughs nervously. "Stocks are taking a tumble." He looks away and scratches his head.

"I hope you've taken care to sell your stock already, sir," I say. A sales pitch is an attempt at making friends long enough to get someone's money. Doing it well is making yourself believe you actually want to be the mark's friend, regardless of the sale. Just temporarily. If you're going to buy a used car, it's understood some jerk in a tartan suit and good dental work is going to do a bad job of pretending to be your friend. And what sort of a deal you get depends on how long you can get the salesman to work to be your friend, until he forgets he doesn't actually *want* to be.

I don't give any sign that I care one way or another. But for all I *do* care, those companies can go down in flames. Sorry, that's not entirely accurate. It's my deepest desire to see these companies fall into the hottest circle of the inferno and try to do business with the other lawyers and hellions who smell fresh meat, and I've been thinking about ways I can help make it happen. They were the cause of my mom getting beaten up (and fired), and me chained to a gurney for almost five weeks.

Before all that happened, Charlie told me that his dad was on the board of directors for the company that I signed a contract with to sell a pint of blood to at regular intervals. It's not clear if they're the people who kidnapped me, but I wouldn't put it past any of them, so in the end who actually did it doesn't really matter.

"Got some people I know, in fact," Charlie's dad continues, his voice turning soft and a tad emotional. "Friends of mine who are sick. Real sick. When I told them about *Blah-Blah-Blah Research Company* finding a cancer cure, they just—" and here's where his eyes get all watery; he takes his handkerchief out, and blows his nose. What a joke. Didn't he take drama class in school?

He staggers his act forward, looking at me all the while. "They just had this hope in their eyes I hadn't seen in years. It was like a load just rolled off their backs."

He's waiting for me to respond with, "Oh, sure, take a vial of my blood and save their lives." But that ain't gonna happen. Not in this lifetime. If he'd come in last week and told me all this, I might have thought about it and felt more predisposed to help his poor, suffering friends. Yeah, I would have fallen for it.

But not now. Not after they spy on my every move and listen to my every word. I take in a deep breath. And everyone I talked to? This is so not good. That puts all my future plans in dire jeopardy. I cuss the inside of my skull blue. I'm not normally profane, not because I'm a saint. But because they're so overused these days they leave the meaning behind. Those with lower IQ levels can spew them out as they wish, but I try to make my words bring more meaning to people. Now, though, it's getting sorta tough trying to figure out what the appropriate words could be without sounding like a hardened, tattoo-covered sailor who wants to grow up and be Blackbeard someday.

So I stare back at Charlie's dad, like a deer in the headlights. I hope he *gets* my act so we can quickly conclude this interrogation. I mean inquest. I mean conversation.

He takes the bait. His face softens. He smiles that smile. *Boy, kid, are you obtuse, so let me make it easy to understand.*

"So, Bernard, what do you think?" he asks.

In a flash I see what he expects. I agree to help his friends and of course they are healed and oh so grateful. Then others hear what happen and also plead to be part of this "miracle." I could be this man's personal real live blood bank. He'd have me all to himself with no middle man. Great plan, huh?

So my drama act commences. Curtains open. Scene one starts.

"About what?" My eyebrows perk up. I still can do the act that passes inspection with my parents. This guy, however, is so much easier. A real pushover.

Maybe I pushed it too far, tugged too hard on his emotional strings. He leans forward, places his hand gently on my shoulder, and smiles.

My reaction? Besides a deep inner revulsion, hidden contempt, and the intense desire to bleach my shoulder? Well, I just look into his eyes with a deeply rehearsed grateful expression as he asks exactly what I expect him to.

"If you donated, say, even a small vial of your blood, I know they'd be…well, beyond grateful." If he was any younger, he'd have puppy dog eyes. But with his gut he's a great big pupper. Doggo territory.

He's said it and now it's all out there, just ready to be thoroughly *discussed*.

Fortunately there are few variables at play here. Three scenarios immediately come to mind.

1. I say, in no uncertain terms, *screw you,* and tell him to leave. He's not getting a drop of my blood, *thankyouverymuch.* After all, it's just so he'll be richer than ever. I can just imagine the auction price this would bring when several companies are desperate to get it. And they'll know he's got *me*. It wouldn't be long before I was once again a prisoner of those blood suckers, unless he's smart enough to keep me constantly on the move. But if I were caught, they'd put me in Maximum Security. No thanks.

While this is the most straightforward and honest option (from my perspective), it could quickly lead to violence, maiming, and pain. Mostly to me. I'm not a wimp. I've taken karate and judo, but that and more recent events (or beatings, if you want to quibble semantics) have just taught me the wisdom of not looking for a fight.

2. I say no firmly politely. I tell him this could cause security leaks and people would track me down and kidnap me again. He would argue that they would never let that happen and no one could know, since they are taking extreme measures to secure my privacy. Yeah, right. I talked to the school's guard, and no one even followed me or asked me what I was doing. Where's the security in that? But I'd argue there's no chance for error and we shouldn't do it. And he'd get all defensive and start his threats, and once again, violence.

3. I say I'm not sure, I hesitate, throw around doubt, fear, and ambiguity. They try to convince me but I can't make up my mind. They give up (for the present) and I don't get hurt.

So you can guess which path I choose. Yep, good 'ol number 3. Foolproof, right?

Seems whenever you make that boast there's a fool just begging to test it.

I prop my elbows on my knees and clasp my hands. I look forlornly down at the floor. Shake my head.

"I'm not sure," I say. I act nervous and throw in a shiver. "I mean, I want to help others, but if anyone finds out I'm here, they'd kidnap me all over again."

Now comes their good-cop bad-cop routine. It's hilarious to watch.

"C'mon, Bernard," Wease whines. "Don't think that way. You know you should help his friends. No one will know. I swear we'll protect you."

Now, Charlie's dad's turn.

His hand returns to my shoulder and I shudder, but not for the reasons he thinks. He figures that I'm this poor, weak-minded adolescent who's lost his family, his direction and, most importantly, his ability to make a decision.

This time his act is better.

"Son," he says paternally. "You've been through a terrible ordeal. Your parents went missing, you were kidnapped, and now you live here, alone. People out there still want to hurt you, but you can trust us to keep you safe no matter what." He gets down on one knee for dramatic effect. Hand stays on the shoulder. "But I *know* you still care about others, like my friends, who desperately need a cure for their broken and bruised bodies. Just a little of your blood can make all the difference in the world. So, what do you say?"

"I still don't know," I whimper. My face is pained as I look into eyes just too caustic at the edges to be sincere. "I'm really confused about who I can trust."

So now Wease, the bad-cop, takes the gloves off, and confirms his involvement in this if I needed a smoking gun; why else would he care?

"How can you say that?" he erupts. "After all we've done for you? Taken you in, sheltered and tutored you? And still you can't trust us? What sort of payback is that?"

Charlie's dad holds up a hand and shakes his head. "Now, Wease," he says. Complacently, like an old grandpa might. "Bernard's been through a lot of trauma, and we can't just expect he'll bounce back after a few days."

Boys and girls, ladies and gentlemen, he got that one right. I'll *never* forget what they did to me. Ever. The stars will burn out first.

Charlie's dad stands, manufactured kindness still radiating from every pore.

"Bernard, I want you to sleep on it tonight. I'll drop by tomorrow and we'll talk again." He holds out his hand and I shake it, disappointed and wishing he was a million miles away right now.

Wease remains to continue the charade of lessons. I half-expect him to follow his master out the door, but they still think I believe them, so I let Wease talk himself up as much as he likes. He mentions helping Charlie's dad indirectly a few more times, but his tone has softened. He even acts sorry over his words. I'm not sure whether I don't believe him or simply don't care.

Fast forward to the end of the school day; why am I having school days as a fugitive again? I almost have to push Wease out the door so I can call my contacts and confirm my "other" arrangements. If things go south tomorrow, I have one day left in this place.

That night I take a walk in the cool darkness. Fog reflects off the elegant lamp posts that are scattered along the path. Out here it reminds me more of an open park instead of a campus, with huge towering shade trees, meandering streams, and concrete bridges. The grass is always cut to golf course-height, and the small hills beckon to my golfing skills, if I had any. Maybe I will gain some, one day.

It's peaceful out among the intermittent gentle breezes. The last rays of sunlight disappear over distant hills. Normally I'd be happy here, but I'm not. The ant nest beneath my conscious thoughts is working furiously to process these new developments. On an intellectual level I'm aware of being valued more as an object than a person, and I've been treated like it already. But the emotional fallout from that fact and the results of it hasn't struck home yet. So there's this emptiness at a core of swirling emotions and thoughts, nothing getting to the point, nothing spinning away to leave me alone. Anger and the need to orchestrate some form of revenge are in a way timeless, but they have to be controlled or else they'll consume me. I had been getting to terms with them until today. The fact that Charlie's dad bugged my new place threw a temporary wrench into that, but I won't let it conquer me.

I'm thinking that I'm making myself the victim here. It should be the other way around. Not that I'd bug their homes. Why go down to their level?

I have cancer curing blood. I have the *cure*, inside my body that many deserving people need. I don't need this place. All I have to do is say when, and I'm gone. But something tells me I should see it through, at least until tomorrow. What will Charlie's dad and Wease's reaction be when I refuse? How will Charlie react when he finds out the truth about both of these nut jobs?

I hop on the campus path again, with purpose taking over. But I also see a different path for *me*, much different than those who want to exploit me.

I walk for about five minutes more, my mind settling, with thoughts of sleep seeping into my head. But just before I turn around to go back to the apartment, who should I see but the female bodyguard, reclining on a metal bench as if waiting for me. I name her *Alexis* since it just seems to fit (Greek meaning is "defender"). She pats the space next to her and I begrudgingly sit with a loud sigh. Instantly the thoughts of my betrayal spring up again. Why does that happen? Why can't I discipline my mind to turn it off?

"Nice night," Alexis says, looking at the stars. We only can see a few because of the lights on campus. But there are some way up and off to her left. She stares at them for a while, with a serene look on her face.

Oh, to have the peace and confidence she has (that right now I could kill for).

"Yeah, sure," I say, rubbing my sore eyes. All at once I feel tired. Very tired. "Great night."

Alexis looks my way. "Tough day with the tutor?"

I shake my head, and the Hoover Dam suddenly bursts. "Tough day after I find out they have cameras in the apartment, spying on me." I rant and rave about how unfair it all is, how the perverts should be rotting in jail. I keep this up for about three minutes until I run out of steam. She's been patiently listening all this time, and so this is where my face starts to burn. I know I should act more grownup instead of throwing a tantrum. I mean, so what? *Strike one* to me.

If they heard about my plans, I should simply change them and move on. Only it's not that simple. *Strike two.*

Plus I want to show her I can handle this stuff without falling apart.

Strike three. I'm out.

I look away, completely embarrassed. She probably doesn't want to have anything more to do with me.

But she takes her turn to talk.

"You don't have any brothers or sisters?"

I shake my head.

She sighs. "I do. A twin sister. Growing up, we shared the same bedroom, she wore my clothes, read *and* wrote in my diary, copied my food likes, you name it. Even talked like me. I had no privacy until we were both out of the house. I wanted to be a private investigator, and so did she. By that time I wanted to be as far away from her as I could, so at the last minute I switched majors. She went on with her own career, and now I have mine. My own place, my own space. Independence. I don't have to share it with anyone I don't want hanging around."

"So?" I ask, confused.

"So?" she says, her eyebrows lifting. "It won't be this way forever. You've signed the contracts. Soon you'll be in your own place and you'll be on your own. Don't sweat it."

I clench my fists. Hard. The anger roars back as my head lowers. "But they—"

She places a hand gently over one of mine, and she shushes me. My anger vanishes in an instant as all sorts of other feelings pour through me. She's probably 10 years my senior. That's too much time, way too much time. Or?

And at that very moment she drops a bombshell.

"You want to know why I wouldn't meet you in your apartment?" she asks slowly. "I knew it was being watched. I stayed away. I saw some techs work in there a couple of days before you arrived. I saw what they were doing, so I disabled the cameras and mics just before you moved in."

I gawk like a gaffed fish and she laughs. Her laugh is lovely. I love everything about her right now.

"They got nothing," she says. "I scanned every inch of that place until everything was turned off. Permanently." She gives me a look of admiration. "How did you figure out they bugged your apartment?"

"Wease and Charlie's dad kept staring at the smoke detectors and outlets," I reply.

She nods. "Probably trying to find some way to fix them. But don't worry. The minute they come back, I'll know. And I'll take care of it." She pauses long enough for the mood to change. "So when do I start? And you read the contract, right? I don't come cheap."

A laugh barks out of me, my entire body relaxes as relief permeates my being. Almost joyful. I feel light, so light I can float home.

My privacy was *not* invaded after all.

"You started when you disabled the cameras and mics," I say.

Did I ever tell you about my awesome bodyguard?

*

Next morning I wake with no nightmare fragments. I feel clean and free, not soiled and chained like yesterday. Bird songs pour through the small window into my bedroom. The fragrance of late spring with its flowers fills the air. I almost sneeze, but manage to hold it in.

*

Wease acts civilly this morning, though he still eyes the smoke detectors and wall outlets from time to time. He even taps them all. It must unnerve him to know he can't do anything about it. He has to act like he knows nothing about their true purpose.

Wease says nothing about the previous day, and even makes an effort to correct my science mistakes with a measure of grace instead of his usual intolerance. Having a family night not too long ago where we watched *Invasion of the Body Snatchers* (the 1958 black and white classic), it makes me wonder about him.

Until Charlie's dad shows up. My heart speeds up now and I wish this was already over with. After further thought it became apparent that there was a fourth and different approach. I'm optimistic that it won't get messy.

Sometimes I don't live in the real world. I'm starting to realize that now.

This time Charlie's dad comes in with his briefcase *and* a supersized box of Dunkin' Donuts: chocolate crème filled, donuts with sprinkles, donut holes, and a few healthy looking muffins (why bother with those, right?). What kid wouldn't soften to all that sugary goodness? I'm beginning to think maybe Charlie's dad isn't a lost cause. Maybe I could bring him over from the Dark Side if that's where he's at.

So there we sit, all super sugar-filled and super sugar high for a few minutes, talking about the weather, politics, and other things that don't matter. Charlie's dad is congenial, supportive, relaxed.

Until he brings up the elephant in the room.

He slaps his legs as he stands.

"So, Bernard, what do you say we help my sick friends? Just a small vial of your blood and they'll be good as new."

I lean back and scratch my belly, grateful for the sugar but not grateful for the change of conversation. Tactic Number Four, you're my only hope. If we had cinnamon buns I could do a Princess Leia impression.

"I've got an idea," I say with a smile. "Give me their names and addresses and I'll take care of it for you. How does that sound?"

"Great! That's great, Bernard!" the balding man says excitedly. But his eyes shift around the room, and his smile weakens. "It's just that, well, time is of the essence." He takes on a downcast look. "I'm not sure how long they are going to last."

I jump to my feet. "All the better to cut out the middle-man. Let's go today," I offer. "No one knows I'm here, and it's a school day. We can leave with the other kids when the bell rings."

I know I'm pushing my luck. If Charlie's dad is smart, he'll play along until we get close to some unknown destination and force my blood from me. But he's going on with this charade because he'd rather I cooperated than use force; we'd part ways right after that. His golden goose will have flown the coop, or wherever it is they fly away from.

"Well...I...I just happen to have what we need right here," he stammers. He opens the briefcase to reveal needles and vials, all ready to go. How convenient. "No need to expose you unnecessarily."

I kick myself, thinking I should have at least considered the fact that he brought that briefcase twice in the last two days. So now it's up to me to think up an excuse why this won't work. My mind goes into action.

"Charlie didn't mention you were a phlebotomist; that's convenient. But what if a vial isn't enough?" I press. "How many friends did you say have cancer?"

"Well...uh," he stalls. "Ten or more."

My gaze flashes across the vials and back to him, nonplussed. "I didn't ask how many vials and spares you brought. I asked how many friends you've got who have cancer. In case you're not sure what a friend is, they'll be listed on your phone's contact list." My patience runs out and my tone shifts to the unacceptable range. "Yesterday you told me how sick your friends were, how they were at death's door, remember? You don't know how many of them there are? Do you even know their names? Are they even real people?"

Oops. Think I said too much there.

It's right there when Wease breaks cover. Up until now he huffs and puffs, showing impatience only too well. He obviously has had enough of this scenario.

"C'mon," he barks to Charlie's dad. "Bernard is just playing you." He looks at me. "Right?"

I shrug with a smile. I'm not gonna lie. There's no point.

"Guilty," I say. "See, we both know there *aren't* any sick friends, but we *do* know that just one vial of my blood will bring you a lot of money."

Charlie's dad's face loses some of its color. But not the man himself. His colors come *shining* through now, and I'm enjoying every second of it.

"You *ungrateful* bastard!" he spits. "I rescued you from the pharm companies and this is the thanks I get?" He towers over me. Or tries. There's functionally not that much difference in height, just width. "And where you gonna go, kid? We got you over a barrel! Where are you gonna hide where they can't find you? Or we can't follow? You got no parents, no home, no friends to help." He pushes a vial in my face. "This'll be worth your while, I can promise you." He hesitates. "We'll even split the money."

"What?" Wease raises his voice an octave. Or maybe two. "That wasn't the deal!"

"Shut up!" Charlie's dad roars, his face turning purple. He grabs Wease by the collar. "You're *worthless*, you know that? Don't have the self-control to keep your trap shut, and now look what happened."

Wease points to me. "Your fault, jerk!" He lunges at me, catching me off guard. I'm pulled to the floor with him on top.

"Get his blood!" Wease screams, and wrestles me down. He outweighs me by about 30 pounds, but I manage a few jabs, making him squirm. Temporarily. He gets me pinned and lays down too close to give me room to wind up. I try whipping an elbow across my chest but it just sinks into the straining muscle of his upper back. No reason not to try a half-dozen more times. He'll have a few prize bruises in the morning, but money is more important than pain to him right now. He just lets out a few grunts and grits his teeth.

It's decision time for Charlie's dad. This is when he has the *one* opportunity to show me he's gonna rise above and do the right thing, or sink into greed.

Only a few milliseconds of indecision pass before he gets the needle and vial ready. Unless he really is a phlebotomist, it dimly occurs to me this is gonna suck on multiple levels.

"Just hold him down!" he shouts, coming down to his knees. "Give me his arm!"

This is not going down like I expected. I should have been ready for Wease's attack, but I was distracted by Charlie's dad ripping into Wease for giving up the game. Was that planned? I twist and writhe, even feeling my lower back pop from the pressure. I kick and yell but Wease uses his weight to hold my hips down; he's in too close to get my legs around his throat and pull him clear.

My left arm is yanked sideways. They hold it down. I fume and grit my teeth.

Suddenly the apartment front door *bangs* once and flies open. My three friends almost fall through it to get inside.

Charlie's dad and Wease pause. They slowly stand. Caught red-handed with me splayed out like a fish ready to be filleted. I can't move much 'cause my back is killing me. But I am enjoying the show.

"Dad?" Charlie cries, his face a picture in sheer horror. "What are you doing to Bernard?"

The man's mouth gapes open, he stutters and stammers and now *he* looks like a deer in the headlights. Seeing his son rapidly losing confidence in him takes its toll and he backs away two steps. Michael and Courtney, my best friends for life, step forward to pull me up, but suddenly Wease pulls out a Taser gun, ready to fire.

Seriously? A tutor with a Taser? That should definitely be illegal. If only because so few would have the patience to refrain from zapping their students every other day.

Michael takes another threatening step forward and Wease goes mad with his newfound power.

"Back off!" he shouts, pointing the Taser at my friends. "Or you'll get this!" He whips around like a snake and, at point-blank range, shoots the Taser right *at my chest.*

I kid you not. What an idiot. That's the way to *kill* me, not just torture to teach me a lesson. Murder one charge coming up for this educated moron.

Of course I get the shock of my life. I stiffen like a board and lose motor control (except for a truncated yelp) as the pain jabs my insides at a thousand punches per second. That's the only way I can explain how it feels. If anyone ever *ever* **ever** offers to tase you so you can prove your machismo, politely decline. Run away, even. You'll thank me for it. It might even save your life.

The shockwave seems to last a lifetime, and if it were fatal I suppose it would, but in reality it's more like five seconds. Wease grins insanely until suddenly, he isn't on top of me anymore. It feels like I should be exhaling smoke with every breath. The chest pain subsides, and I slowly bring myself up to my elbows to see Alexis handcuffing him and jerk him to his feet. At least his nose is bleeding. Too bad other parts aren't.

The other school bodyguards pour in and quickly secure the apartment. One snatches the Taser gun that was kicked to the floor, while the other guard arrests Charlie's dad. Apparently these guys have police authority and aren't afraid to use it. As Alexis reads Wease his rights, another does the same for Charlie's dad.

Charlie just sits down and cries.

After Alexis pushes Wease over to another guard, she supports my shoulders.

"You okay?" she asks.

"You're late," I say. My lower back aches but I think I'm coming out of it, but just as fast, I'm not feeling it any more. Sweat flows from my pores, all over, and I shake. A headache takes over and nausea follows. Alexis tries to lift me to my feet, but I slide through her arms and sink to the floor. It gets worse: the inside of my chest hurts this time, bad enough to keep me from breathing. I curl up into a fetal position, close my eyes, and fade away.

*

I wake in a hospital bed, with tubes all over me, and the first thing I look at are my wrists. I sigh, relieved they aren't cuffed to a gurney. I'm in a private room, much nicer than my apartment could ever be. Alexis sits on my right, watching me carefully, with arms folded. On the other chairs sit my friends (Charlie lays sideways in his), looking at the floor, sleeping or texting.

My chest still burns, but this time it's only skin-deep. No, wait. My ribs are sore, too. Are they broken? When did that happen? I look inside my gown to see a hefty scar just above a chest wrap.

And it all comes back. *Wease tried to kill me* with a stupid Taser. Wow, I guess I didn't think of as many options as I should have. Next time I'll use my karate first, followed by a few knockout judo kicks. Scratch that. I'll get my butt to the gym first so technique won't be outclassed by weight.

Alexis leans over and looks me in the eye. Her auburn hair, usually impeccably straight and styled, sticks out at the sides. She's still in her work clothes, now mostly wrinkled and dirty from the scuffle. Light bags beneath her eyes tell me she's been up a while.

"Sorry I didn't get to you sooner," she says. "We had some *questionables* try to break in the school. I think they were looking for you." She looks over at Michael, Courtney, and Charlie. "They've been here all day."

"What happened?" I ask. I knew it must have been from the Taser, but I wanted to hear it out loud. "Why did I end up here?"

"Cardiac arrhythmia," Alexis replies.

I look at her. I know what cardiac means—something to do with the heart. But arrhythmia? That doesn't sound good.

"Did I have a heart attack?" I ask softly. I breathe in deeply, feeling my sore ribs again. They hurt. Lower back still aches, too.

By this time my friends wake up/stir, and instantly gather on my left. Michael and Courtney smile at me, but not Charlie. His face is serious, his gaze down.

"Heart attack?" Michael asks. "That's putting it mildly. You were like—oh, *gasp—can't breathe...choke...choke. My chest hurts*. Pass out." He falls to the floor and I give him extra points for being dramatic. His being a jackass is comforting; I can't bring to mind what would make him take things seriously but it would have to be bad.

"Yeah," Courtney says. "Your heart stopped." She looks at Alexis. "But thanks to your personal bodyguard, you're here." Her gaze returns to me, brow furrowing. "You didn't say anything about hiring her."

"Everything happened fast," I say, and try for a helpless shrug, then stop when my ribs shriek. "Didn't get the chance to tell you guys."

Michael is all grins. His arms are folded.

"What?" I ask.

"You should have seen how Alexis brought you back. She was a *pro*."

I swallow. I'm feeling warm. "You mean...CPR?"

He nods. "Chest compressions *and* mouth-to-mouth. It was awesome." Michael laughs.

Alexis turns to Michael as Courtney elbows him fiercely. Her expression flashes from the quick assessment to the long-suffering dismissal of a lioness hearing a challenge and ignoring it as the play-fighting of juvenile males. Michael steps back a pace with a reddened face. "I mean, real professional," he adds. But he's still wearing that stupid grin. Alexis' eyes roll heavenward.

I feel my face burn. She brought me back to life? Wow. Now I really owe her.

Charlie rubs at his eyes. They're leaking.

"Sorry...I'm sorry," he mumbles. "About my dad. That jerk."

"Not your fault," I say.

"We can't choose blood," Alexis says. She remains impassive, but I'm beginning to suspect she's got a wicked sense of humor.

"I should have known," Charlie replies. "Never should have trusted him. He only wanted the money."

"Both he and your tutor are facing jail time," Alexis says to me. "I pressed charges for you. You may have to appear in court."

"Fine with me," I say. "Wease deserves whatever's coming to him."

Alexis nods. "Attempted murder of a minor might lock him away for a good while."

Charlie keeps wiping at his eyes. I feel for him because of his dad.

"Your father will have some good lawyers," I console. "They might just let him go with a slap on the wrist."

"Th-that's the problem," he stutters. "I don't care if he goes to jail. He d-deserves it." He pauses as his face twists. "But we won't have money for my school after his lawyers represent him. He's already told me that. I probably won't even be able to finish out the term."

Good ol' Charlie. A solid friend who was there to help me out of a big dark spot. And now he has to pay for his father's erroneous ways? How can I just leave him hanging like that?

I can't.

I won't do that to my friends.

Ever.

"Is that what you're bawling about?" I say with more enthusiasm than my aching ribs should allow. "Man, greed is the whole reason this mess started, and it would be hypocritical of me to act the same as the corporate bastards who would bleed me dry and charge sick people their souls for the cure. As far as I'm concerned, anything I've got is yours to use; you've already shown me that you'd give me your last dime if I needed it. I'll pay the rest of your high school tuition. If things get bad at home, stay on campus if you want."

"Serious?" he says, brightening through his watery eyes.

"Yep," I say, and he gives me a high-five. His tears flow again, but big happy ones this time. He laughs, and assures me that campus life will be his definite preferred choice. I promise to make all the arrangements. Alexis promises she'll make them for me. I have no clue who promises her they'll make them for her.

Maybe she handles things herself. Another point in her favor.

*

The doctor comes in, talks with Alexis, and she escorts everyone out of the room, including herself. The man is in his mid-thirties, professional. Short, black hair and beginning to bald just a little. Good looking as far as doctors go. Alexis must have paid through the nose to get him to come and check on me in a timely manner.

He seems to know something I don't. He washes up in the sink, and has yet to talk to me, which in itself isn't out of the ordinary. But considering my circumstances there are more dark alleys my imagination can get yanked into and mugged than if I were here because I had a runny nose. Is something wrong? Is the doctor gonna go *hey, this was all a joke. Your blood really doesn't cure cancer. In fact you have it. Sorry, kid.*

But he turns to me.

"So, you're really him, eh?"

I take a long breath let it out slow. Feel my body relax again. Maybe I'm not gonna die just yet.

"I'm me," I say quietly.

The doctor smiles, shakes his head, and gently takes my wrist and hesitates.

"The Cancer Cure Kid. You've heard that, right?" He places his hands on my face and moves my head back and forth.

I shake my head.

"Amazing. No sign of it anywhere."

Now I'm confused.

"What's amazing?"

"First one to be cured with the new cancer drug, right? The one everyone's talking about? You were kidnapped, disappeared? And now you end up here with a heart attack."

I snort derisively. "What?" I shout, feeling some major irritation coming my way. *Change the tone*, I tell myself. *He knows nothing about what's going on.* I hyperventilate a few more breaths. I feel calmer. "Cardiac arrhythmia," I say. "It wasn't a heart attack."

"Thanks for clarifying," he says wryly. "Glad one of us is a doctor to keep these things in order." He pulls up a stool beside me. The humor dappling his features damps; he's perplexed. "So why is everyone hunting you up?"

"Hunting me down," I say.

"Like I said," he replies evenly, "glad one of us is educated."

It's clear I'm more beaten up than I realized. An obvious trap like that would've never got me under normal circumstances. It's not admitted anything yet, aside from telling me that he's a lot smarter than Charlie's dad and knows he's being lied to, but doesn't know what part of the story is a lie. He's curious and intelligent, sharp as a tack, but there's nothing predatory about him. Still, I'm not at my best right now.

I stare holes into him. *Who else knows*, I wonder. Is someone coming after me, right now, to take me away? Did someone pay this doctor to hold me here until they arrive?

"Where's Alexis?" I ask.

"Your sister?" the doc says. "I sent her out. Doctor's prerogative."

"I know what you did. The question is why. Alexis is my bodyguard."

This seems to amuse the doctor and he gives me a slight smile. He leans back and folds his arms, now staring holes into *me*. He scratches his head and leans forward.

"Okay, so I'm only getting part of a picture here, and I'm hoping you can fill me in on the details. I see your mug shot all over the news. Someone kidnapped the Cancer Cure Kid, and everyone's worried that you'll end up dead in some garbage bin. You show up here, having survived a Taser gun, and the one you call your bodyguard says I'm on a need-to-know basis. If I want anything, I have to ask you. Doesn't add up." He leans back. "You're a minor, so by law we're required to report the assault. Why shouldn't I call the police right now?"

I try to choose my words carefully. Very very carefully.

"I could ask you a few questions."

The man looks agreeable and nods.

"When you saw the news, which pharm company was being interviewed?"

"The *Blah Blah Blah Research Company.*"

So that's how they covered this up, making me out to be the patient who was cured, but afterward kidnapped. They could delay the "cure," citing risks to those who take it. Thus giving themselves more time to find me. And what unsuspecting doctor or nurse wouldn't be happy to be the hero who finds, and turns over, this poor, lost, Cancer Cure Kid?

I refuse to hide in all this, perpetuating the lie. But I know I have to do this right, beginning with my tone. If I sound all freaked out, it will all go backward. Or downward.

I take a deep breath, grimacing at my hurting ribs.

"A reasonable man would know," I say as gently as I can, "you shouldn't believe everything you see on the news."

The doctor's eyes brighten and he nods. "The *Blah Blah Blah Research Company* certainly doesn't have a sterling reputation. So try me."

"Are you sure?" I say as an idea suddenly hits me. Without waiting for him to respond I ask, "Where's the nearest cancer research hospital?"

The doc shakes his head. "Let's back up and have you tell me your story. After that I'll answer your question."

"Fair enough," I say, pushing the button that lifts the bed. Despite my protesting ribs and back, I prefer this position. So I can talk to this man eye-to-eye. Who knows? Maybe he can even help.

"*I* am the cancer cure," I say flatly, with no emotion. "I gave blood on my 16th birthday to the Red Cross. Titer levels were through the roof and a researcher got a hold of some of it and tested it directly on cancerous cells; exposed it to dozens of strains."

I stop there, allowing this to soak in. I'm sure he doesn't believe me. I mean, who would? But he looks a little more than just intrigued. His eyes widens for one thing, and he leans forward.

"And?" he asks, his tone rising.

I smack my hand in fist.

"Killed it all. Even the stem cells."

The doctor smiles. I've seen that kind of smile before. It's like, *Okay, kid, where's the punchline?*

"This isn't a joke," I continue. "The *Blah Blah Blah Research Company* won the contract for my blood, leaving the others in the dust. One loser company came after me and they haven't stopped since."

"*Contracted*...for your blood? Do you even know how implausible that sounds?" the man says.

"You know pharm companies better than the public," I shoot back. "You should know how plausible it is. Heck, you can look up all the testing they do in countries where it would be legal if they accidentally poisoned and killed subjects in the process. That's an accepted practice. What do you think they wouldn't do for a golden ticket?"

He doesn't react. Obviously I'm not convincing him, but I don't have to. He might just be one more greedy pawn in the pockets of one of the pharm companies. I don't know him.

But, true to his word, he tells me the name of the nearest cancer research hospital. And of course it has to local. Can't I ever be rid of this town? He also writes the name of a doctor I should get in touch with if I'm ever over that way: Maxwell Looney.

I thank him and ask him to bring Alexis back in. He does so, but first he talks to her for a while out in the hall, but I can't make out much more than the word *bodyguard*. Hey, I never said she *wasn't* my sister. When they return, the doc gives me a straight face.

"You are free to leave anytime," he says. And just like that, he turns and leaves. No good-byes or good-lucks or the typical well-wishing that docs normally do. I figure he was just too busy to stick around any longer.

Really hoping he wrote a script for something in my discharge notes, or so my ribs say in aching promise every time I take a deep breath.

*

My friends gather in close. They understand it will only endanger their welfare if they know where I am. Charlie's eyes start watering again. He says he feels guilty about what happened, and still blames himself for trusting his dad. All of us tell him repeatedly that it's not his fault, but I don't think we got through to him. I just hope he'll be okay.

Alexis, as my newly hired personal bodyguard, takes charge of my assigned wheelchair and tails it into the hallways, through the corridors and out the main hospital door. I slowly and painfully stand and give high-fives to Michael, a hug to Courtney (who kisses me on the cheek), and a side hug to Charlie. I watch as they leave to the parking lot and send me a final wave before taking off.

This sucks. There goes another part of my family. Why am I being pulled apart from everyone I know? Life is not getting any better. It's still going backward.

Alexis looks at me. "Your car is on the way."

Thirty seconds later, a red BMW-1, brand new, pulls beside the curb. I slide in the front passenger's side and give a fist bump to the young driver, a professional NASCAR racer who can lose anyone on the road, and I mean *anyone*. I can't tell you his real name (I call him Rex, Speed Racer's older brother), but he's like 007-brilliant as a chauffeur.

Why hire a driver, you ask? Especially a pro racecar driver? Because you can't be too careful when you're on the road these days.

*

We've been on the road for over two hours, and no one is following. I think we're getting close to the "new place" because I can see ocean, and our road has narrowed to a single, winding lane, which curves so often that I'm nauseated, even though I'm still sitting up front. I am not a good backseat passenger, even on a straightaway.

Another day is almost done, but I can just make out the house ahead on the gray sandy shore. My heart skips a few beats as we near my three-story, ten bedroom beach house. Did I tell you my awesome bodyguard is also fluent in working with professionals who handle money? Especially offshore accounts?

Yep, all this is mine. Comes with a pool, a few acres of beaches and private woods, a cook/maid and even a new tutor when school starts in the fall. Plenty of room for all, even for you if you come to visit. Maybe that can happen. Someday.